Quiet in the Library

Paul Shipton
Illustrated by Tony Ross

Miss Miggs worked in the library.

The library was a quiet
place to work.

A woman came in to the library.
She made a noise.

"Please be quiet," said
Miss Miggs.

A man came in to the library.

He made a noise.

"Please be quiet," said
Miss Miggs.

A girl came in to the library.
She made a noise.

"Please be quiet," said
Miss Miggs.

A boy came in to the library.
He made a noise.

"Please be quiet," said
Miss Miggs.

At the end of the day, Miss Miggs went home.

She made LOTS of noise.

15

"**Please be quiet!**" everyone said.